Birthday Book Club

This book has been donated by

ANNE & RONALD KOHL

in honor of

ALEXANDRA KOHL 's

third _____ **birthday**

HANS CHRISTIAN ANDERSEN

Thumbelina

Retold and illustrated by

Lauren Mills

LITTLE, BROWN AND COMPANY

New York ⁓ Boston

There was once a widow who longed for a little child of her own, and so she went to a wise witch and begged her, "Oh, please can you tell me how I might find a child?"

"Find a child? *Pfff!* Nothing is easier. The village streets are lined with them!" teased the witch.

"Yes, but I would like to have a little one I can call my own," said the widow. "Can't you help me?"

"Well, maybe I can and maybe I can't," replied the witch. "Take this barleycorn. Now mind you, it's no ordinary seed. Plant it during the new moon and see what happens!"

"Oh, thank you!" said the widow, and handed her a coin. Then she went straight home and waited for the new moon. No sooner had she planted the barleycorn than a lovely tulip began to grow, with petals shut tight.

"Ah, well," said the widow, "it's no child, but at least it's a pretty flower," and she kissed the petals.

But just then, *POP!*, the flower burst open, and there in the center sat a tiny girl who was not even as big as the woman's thumb. And so the old widow named her Thumbelina.

The widow fashioned a polished walnut shell for Thumbelina's bed, with violet petals for her mattress and rose petals for her blankets. During the day Thumbelina played by the window, where the woman had set a bowl ringed by a garland of flowers. Thumbelina liked to sit on a large tulip petal and row herself back and forth, using two white horsehairs for oars. As she played, she sang in the sweetest voice the widow had ever heard.

By and by the witch stopped in to see how the widow and her tiny child were getting along. "Are you happy now?" the witch asked the widow.

"Yes, except for one thing," the old widow answered. "I watch that Thumbelina is safe at all times, but I know that someday I will die and there will be no one to look out for her."

The wise witch, who was quite old herself, nodded and said, "I know something about caring for children. Someday they start to take care of themselves, but only after you've let them go. You will know when it is time for Thumbelina to leave you. At that time you must open the window to the world and let be what is to be."

And so there came a time when the widow noticed that Thumbelina was no longer playing happily at her old games. Instead, she sat listlessly on the windowsill gazing out at the butterflies fluttering about freely. One night when Thumbelina was sleeping in her bed, the widow quietly opened the window, bent down, and gently kissed Thumbelina for the last time.

A crescent moon rose and shone its light upon Thumbelina, and a toad hopping by caught sight of her. "What a nice wife she would make for my son!" croaked the toad, and she hopped right in through the open window! She snatched up the walnut bed with the sleeping Thumbelina inside and hopped off with it down to the garden.

By the garden there flowed a brook, and it was here amid the muddy banks that the toad lived with her son. *"Croaky-croak-croak!"* was all the son could say when he saw the pretty maiden sleeping.

"*Shh!* Not so loud or you'll wake her," said the mother toad. "She could run away too easily, for she's as light as swansdown. We'll put her on one of the lily pads far from shore where she can't escape. In the meantime, we can fix up the best room under the mud, where you two will live together."

When the old toad and her son had finished preparing the wedding chamber, they swam out to greet Thumbelina. The mother toad curtsied and said, "Allow me to introduce my son to you. He is to be your husband, and we shall all live together in our lovely home in the mud."

"Croaky-croak-croak!" was all the son could add. Then they fetched Thumbelina's walnut bed and swam off with it to the new bridal chamber.

Thumbelina sat alone on the green leaf and wept. She had no desire to live in the mud with the toads, but the toads cared nothing at all for what she wanted.

The little fish in the water who had seen and heard all that had happened popped their heads up to take a closer peek at Thumbelina. When they saw how sad she was they decided to help her escape. Swarming around the green stalk of the lily pad, they nibbled on it until the leaf broke free. It floated quietly downstream, carrying Thumbelina safely away from the toads, but also farther from her home.

Thumbelina sailed on and on past many places, all the while listening to the birds singing sweetly to her. For a time, a dainty butterfly fluttered about her, and Thumbelina was overjoyed for its company and for the brilliant sun shining down on the water, which glittered like liquid gold.

Thumbelina's happiness soon ended when a big beetle swooped down and clasped its claws around her waist and flew up with her into a tree. He settled himself next to the terrified girl, fed her some nectar from the blossoms of the tree, and told her that she was very pretty, although she looked nothing like a beetle.

Before long all the other beetles that lived in the tree came to pay a visit. Two lady beetles examined Thumbelina with their antennae and scornfully announced, "She has only two legs and no antennae!" Another said, "And neither has she wings! Ugh! She looks almost human!"

"Oh! How ugly!" called out all the other beetles.

The beetle who had carried her off still thought she was pretty, but since the others were in agreement that she was the ugliest thing they'd ever seen, he kept quiet. He finally decided to have nothing to do with her, and so he carried her down to a daisy on the forest floor and left her there.

Thumbelina wondered if indeed she was as ugly as the beetles said. It was her luck, however, that they were so shortsighted, for how miserable she would have been if she had been made to live among them.

All summer long Thumbelina lived alone in that enormous wood. She wove herself a bed of grass and hung it under a large dock leaf to protect herself from the rain. She ate from the nectar of the flowers and drank from the dew on the leaves.

Every day at sunrise and at sunset, Thumbelina searched the
horizon for her mother, who she thought might be looking for
her, but no one came. The summer passed and the fall.

*T*hen came winter, the long, cold winter. All the birds who had sung so sweetly had now flown away; the trees dropped their leaves; the flowers died. Her dock-leaf canopy had shriveled up and withered to a yellow stalk.

Thumbelina felt bitterly cold, for by this time her clothes were in tatters. It began to snow, and since she was so tiny every snowflake that fell upon her felt like a huge shovelful. She wrapped herself in a dead leaf, but there was little warmth in that.

On the edge of the wood lay a large cornfield with only the bare stubble standing above the frozen ground. This made an entire forest for her to walk through, and it was here she looked for shelter.

At last she came to the door of a lady field mouse who lived warm and snug underground, with a storeroom full of grain, a cozy kitchen, and a parlor. Poor Thumbelina stood outside the door as forlorn and hungry as could be.

"Oh, you poor girl!" said the field mouse. "Come inside my warm home and share my dinner."

The old field mouse took a liking to Thumbelina, and said, "You're quite welcome to stay with me for the winter as long as you keep my rooms nice and tidy and tell me stories, for I'm so fond of them." And Thumbelina did as the field mouse asked and felt quite comfortable there.

"I daresay we shall have a visitor soon," said the field mouse one day. "My neighbor generally pays me a visit once a week. He is even better off than I am. He has a much finer house, and goes about in a splendid black velvet coat. If only you could get him for a husband, you would be well taken care of. But his eyesight is very bad. You must tell him all your best stories."

This neighbor was a mole, and Thumbelina was not at all pleased with the notion of marrying him. The next day he paid them a visit in his black velvet coat.

He was also well educated, according to the field mouse, but he couldn't stand sunshine or flowers. He poked all sorts of fun at them, never having seen them.

Thumbelina had to sing to him, so she sang both "Ladybug, Ladybug, Fly Away Home" and "Ring Around the Rosies" so beautifully that the mole fell in love with her; but he wouldn't say, as he was much too cautious a mole for that.

The mole had lately dug a long underground tunnel from his house to theirs and invited the field mouse and Thumbelina to stroll there as they pleased. He told them, however, not to be afraid of the dead bird that lay in the passage.

The mole took a bit of touchwood in his mouth, for it shines in the dark just like fire, and went ahead to give them light. When they came to where the dead bird lay, Thumbelina could see it was a pretty swallow with its head and legs tucked in between its feathers. The poor bird must have died from the cold and fallen into the mole's tunnel. Thumbelina felt sorry for it, for she dearly loved the birds who had sung so sweetly all summer long. But the mole kicked at it and said, "Now it will twitter no more! How wretched it must be to be born a bird! A bird like that has nothing but its twittering, and then he's sure to starve to death when winter comes."

"Just what I would expect to hear from a sensible mole like you," said the field mouse. "What does a bird have with all its singing when it's only bound to starve and freeze?"

Thumbelina didn't say a word, but when the other two had turned their backs to the swallow, she bent down and brushed aside the feathers from his head and kissed his closed eyes gently. *Perhaps it was he who sang so sweetly in the summer,* she thought.

That night Thumbelina crept from her bed and wove a nice big blanket of hay, which she carried down and spread over the dead swallow, and she took some soft thistledown that she had found in the field mouse's storeroom and tucked this in at his sides so that the bird might lie warm in the cold earth.

"Good-bye, dear bird," she said, "and thank you for your beautiful singing last summer when the sun shone warmly on us." She laid her head on the bird's breast. Just then she quickly jumped back in fright, for she heard a thumping inside! It was the swallow's heart! The bird was not dead at all, only numb and unconscious.

Thumbelina trembled in fright, for the bird was so large beside her. She gathered courage, however, and tucked thistledown still more closely around the poor swallow and fetched her own bedcover and spread this over the bird.

The next night she crept out again to the swallow and found him alive but very weak.

"Thank you, dear girl," the sick swallow said to her. "I am so wonderfully warm now. I shall soon get my strength back and will be able to fly again, out into the sunshine!"

"Oh, no!" Thumbelina said. "It's snowing outside. Stay in your warm bed and I will take care of you."

Then she brought him water in a flower petal, which he drank. Afterward he told her how he had torn his wing on a bramble, so that he could not keep up with the other swallows when they flew away to the warm countries. At last he had fallen to the ground, but he could remember no more.

All winter long the swallow stayed there, and Thumbelina took care of him. Neither the mole nor the field mouse knew anything about it.

When spring arrived, Thumbelina opened the hole in the roof for the swallow. The warm sun shone upon them, and the swallow asked Thumbelina if she would come away with him, for she could sit on his back. Thumbelina wanted very much to fly away, but she knew her disappearance would grieve the field mouse. Besides, she still wondered if her mother might find her.

"No, I cannot," said Thumbelina.

"Good-bye, then, you dear sweet girl," said the swallow, and he flew toward the open sunshine. Thumbelina gazed after him with tears filling her eyes, for she was so fond of the swallow.

*E*very morning as the sun rose and every evening as it set Thumbelina went out and searched across the cornfield to see if her mother might be looking for her. When the corn above the field mouse's burrow had grown high into the air, making a thick forest again, Thumbelina was very sad. She was no longer allowed to go out into the warm sunshine.

"You must prepare for your wedding," the field mouse told her, "for our neighbor, the mole, has finally made his marriage proposal. How lucky for a poor girl like you! Now, you will need both woolens and linens if you are to be the mole's wife."

Thumbelina had to spend all her days spinning, and the field mouse also hired four strong spiders to help spin and weave. Each evening the mole would visit and go on and on about how awful the sun was now when it scorched the earth, making it hard as stone and difficult for him to dig. After the summer was over, he would have his wedding with Thumbelina. But she was not at all pleased, for she found the mole to be a terrible bore.

Whenever she could, Thumbelina would slip out the door. When the wind parted the ears of corn so that she could glimpse the blue sky, then she thought of how beautiful and bright it was out there, and wished to see the dear swallow just once more. But the swallow never came; certainly he had flown far away, far into the beautiful green forest.

utumn arrived, and Thumbelina's wedding things were ready. "Tomorrow you will be married!" the field mouse said to her. Poor Thumbelina wept and said she could not marry the boring mole.

"*Piff, sniff!*" said the field mouse. "Don't be so stubborn, or I'll bite you with my sharp teeth. He's a fine husband, he is. The Queen herself hasn't anything to compare with that black velvet coat. His kitchen and cellar are full, and you should be thankful for that."

That night Thumbelina peered out the mouse's doorway and glanced up at the half-moon. "Oh, lovely moon," she said, "how you look like the bowl I once played in when I had a mother. Do not tell my mother how sad I am, for then she would grieve even more." Thumbelina crept off to bed. When at last sleep came, her mother visited her in a dream and said, "Dear Thumbelina, you can never make others happy unless you yourself are happy."

The next morning the mole came to fetch Thumbelina. She would have to live with him down under the earth and never come into the warm sunshine, for that he could not stand. Thumbelina was so full of sorrow, because she now had to part from the beautiful sun!

She begged the field mouse and mole to allow her to say one last farewell to the sun, and they allowed her to do so.

"Good-bye, dear sun," she said sadly, and boldly took a few steps outside, then a few more. The corn had once again been cut and the sun shone down brightly. "Good-bye," she said, throwing her arms around a little red flower that stood near. "Remember me to the dear swallow, if you chance to see him."

"*Tweet, tweet!*" she suddenly heard above her. She looked up and there was the swallow, just overhead. As soon as he saw Thumbelina he was delighted. She told her old friend how unwilling she was to marry the boring mole and live deep underground where the sun never shone. As she spoke she could not stop from crying.

"The cold winter is coming," said the swallow, "and I am flying far away to warmer lands. Won't you come with me, where the sun shines even more brightly than it does here, where it is always summery and there are beautiful flowers? Do come with me, dear Thumbelina, who saved my life!"

"Yes, I will go now and find my own happiness!" Thumbelina said, and climbed on the swallow's back. She tied her sash to one of his strong feathers, and up the swallow flew, high into the air, over the woods and over the sea, high up above the tall mountains where the snow forever lies. When Thumbelina was cold she snuggled down under his warm feathers, putting her head out now and then to see all the beauty of the world beneath her.

At last they reached the warm land, where the sun shone more brightly than Thumbelina had ever seen. The sky seemed twice as high, and in the hedges grew the finest grapes; in the groves hung oranges and lemons; the air smelled sweetly of myrtle and curled mint; and happy children darted about on the paths.

But the swallow kept flying on and on, and the country became more and more beautiful. Then, under leafy green trees and beside a blue lake, stood an ancient castle built of gleaming white marble. Vines twisted around the high pillars. On the topmost of these were many swallows' nests, and in one of them dwelt the swallow who was carrying Thumbelina.

"Here is my house!" said the swallow. "But if you would rather have a home of your own, all you need to do is choose one of the beautiful flowers that grows below, and I will set you there."

"That would be wonderful!" exclaimed Thumbelina.

The swallow flew down with Thumbelina and set her upon one of the broad petals of an exquisite white flower. But how astonished she was! There in the middle of the flower sat a little man, just Thumbelina's size. He wore a splendid crown on his head and had bright wings on his shoulders.

The fairy king was terrified of the swallow, for in comparison to him the bird seemed gigantic. Even so, he boldly stood guard over the flowers and did not move.

"Oh my goodness, how noble he is," whispered Thumbelina to the swallow.

When the king caught sight of Thumbelina he was delighted, for she had the kindest face he had ever seen, and certainly she was the bravest maiden he had ever known. And so he took his crown from his head and placed it on hers, asking to know her name and whether she would be his wife. If so, she would be queen of all the flowers.

Yes, he would make a proper sort of husband for her, different from a toad's son or a beetle or a mole. And yes, she thought she had learned enough of the world to understand what makes a wise queen.

So she said yes to the noble king, and out from every flower
stepped a lady or gentleman so charming that it was a
pleasure to see them. Each brought Thumbelina a present, but the
best of all was a beautiful pair of wings that were fastened to her
back, so now she too could fly from flower to flower.

"As free as the butterflies!" exclaimed Thumbelina, who had
found her happiness.

*T*he swallow sat above in his nest and sang to them as well as he could, but his heart was full of sorrow, for he was fond of Thumbelina and did not want to be parted from her. But in time, he too rejoiced, knowing that Thumbelina was always meant to be queen of all the flowers. And so he sang her story wherever he went.

For Evie and all the adventures ahead

I would like to thank my editor Maria Modugno, husband Dennis Nolan, daughter Evie Nolan, and aunt Marcy Deets. Thanks also to Amy Hsu, Paige Davis, Alison Impey, Sara Morling, Christine Cuccio, Cynthia Kane, Bill Horton, Mary Lawler, and all the wonderful librarians at Meekins Library.

Copyright © 2005 by Lauren Mills

All rights reserved.

Little, Brown and Company • Time Warner Book Group • 1271 Avenue of the Americas, NY, NY 10020

Visit our Web site at www.lb-kids.com

First Edition

Library of Congress Cataloging-in-Publication Data

Mills, Lauren A.
    Hans Christian Andersen's Thumbelina / retold and illustrated by Lauren Mills. — 1st ed.
      p. cm.
    Summary: After being kidnapped by a toad, a beautiful girl no bigger than a thumb has a series of dreadful experiences and makes many animal friends before meeting a fairy prince just her size.
   ISBN 0-316-57359-0
    [1. Fairy tales.] I. Title: Thumbelina. II. Andersen, H. C. (Hans Christian), 1805–1875. Thumbelina. III. Title.

PZ8.M635 Han 2003
398.2—dc21
[E]   2002022491

10 9 8 7 6 5 4 3 2 1

Book design by Lauren Mills and Alison Impey

SC

Manufactured in China

The illustrations for this book were done in watercolor on Arches paper.
The text was set in Diotima and Ariadne, and the display type is hand-lettered by Mary Lawler.

J
398.2
M   Mills, Lauren A.   # 16.99

          Thumbelina.

DATE		
FEB 1 3 2008		
AUG 1 5 2007		
APR 0 8 2011		

LO: 4/11
ØX11
ØP+3

9/05

BAKER & TAYLOR